To the power of love, activism, and standing up for equality. Thank you, Edie, Thea, and Robbie, and every single voice that has ever fought for fairness. —M. G.

To my wife, Bianca —C. T.

Text copyright © 2025 by Michael Genhart
Illustrations copyright © 2025 by Cheryl Thuesday
All rights reserved. No part of this book may be reproduced, transmitted, or stored in an information retrieval system in any form or by any means, electronic, mechanical, photocopying, recording, or otherwise, without written permission from the publisher.
LEE & LOW BOOKS INC., 381 Park Avenue South, New York, NY 10016
leeandlow.com

Edited by Jessica V. Echeverria
Book design by John Candell
Book production by The Kids at Our House
The text is set in Josefin Sans
The illustrations are created digitally in Fresco, Illustrator, and Photoshop, and good ole pencil and paper.

Manufactured in China by RR Donnelley
1 3 5 7 9 10 8 6 4 2
First Edition

Library of Congress Cataloging-in-Publication Data
Names: Genhart, Michael, author. | Thuesday, Cheryl, illustrator.
Title: Edie for equality : Edie Windsor stands up for love / by Michael Genhart ; illustrated by Cheryl Thuesday.
Description: First edition. | New York : Lee & Low Books Inc., [2025] | Includes bibliographical references. | Audience: Ages 7-13 | Summary: "A picture book biography of LGBTQ icon Edie Windsor, who made history when she sued the US government for discrimination, in case United States v. Windsor, which helped overturn the Defense of Marriage Act (DOMA). Includes timeline, bibliographical references, and photos"–Provided by publisher.
Identifiers: LCCN 2024023081 | ISBN 9781643795829 (hardback) | ISBN 9781643795836 (ebk)
Subjects: LCSH: Windsor, Edie–Juvenile literature. | Same-sex marriage–United States–Juvenile literature. | Same-sex marriage–Law and legislation–United States–Juvenile literature. | Gay rights–United States–Juvenile literature.
Classification: LCC HQ1034.U5 G46 2025 | DDC 306.84/8–dc23/eng/20241009
LC record available at https://lccn.loc.gov/2024023081

The facts in the text were accurate and all hyperlinks were live at the time of the book's original publication. The author and publisher do not assume any responsibility for changes made since that time.

"America's long journey towards equality has been guided by countless small acts of persistence, and fueled by the stubborn willingness of quiet heroes to speak out for what's right.

Few were as small in stature as Edie Windsor—and few made as big a difference to America."

—PRESIDENT BARACK OBAMA

This is a story about a great unfairness and how Edie Windsor stood up for what was right.

But Edie wasn't always someone who was bold.

She was a girl who played by the rules.

Except for the times she got kicked out of the movie theater for making her own music.

In school, Edie loved math.
Numbers added up just so, and there was always a correct answer.
Equal meant equal.
Edie also liked her civics class, where she learned about important laws and treating people fairly.

Edie thought a little more fairness in the neighborhood would be a good idea.

Especially when neighbors said mean things to her family because they were Jewish.

In college, Edie started to discover something big about herself: she had romantic feelings for other women. Yet everyone and everything around her said she was supposed to be with a man. Edie didn't think this was fair, but she knew that people were going to jail for being gay or lesbian, so she kept her feelings a secret.

That's why Edie decided to move to New York City, where it would be easier to be herself. There she landed a job as a computer programmer. At the time, she was the only woman in her department. Edie stood out.

Like Edie, Thea knew about unfairness.
She was forced to flee her home in Europe during wartime with her Jewish family.
When she was in college, Thea was kicked out for kissing another woman.
She later became a psychologist, to help others who had been hurt like her.

But when she met Edie, her life filled with joy.
It wasn't long before Edie and Thea fell in love. How happy they were!

At parties and beach gatherings, they danced and danced. The merengue, the Lindy Hop, the hully gully . . .

One day Thea got down on one knee and asked, "Edie Windsor, will you marry me?"

Edie shouted, "Yes! Yes! Yes!" and proudly wore the round diamond pin Thea gave her.

While men and women couples could celebrate their engagements by showing off their rings and throwing parties, Edie and Thea could not. They did not want anyone asking, "Who's the lucky guy?" Also, it was against the law for two women or two men to get married.

This unfairness didn't stop Edie and Thea from enjoying their life together. They traveled the world, cooked up favorite meals, and splashed in the waves during summers by the seaside.

Then in June 1969, Edie and Thea learned that there had been an uprising at the Stonewall Inn, a gathering place for gay people. At that time, police frequently arrested drag queens, lesbians, and gay and transgender people just for being themselves. But this time people got really angry and fought back—a fight that would last several days and nights.

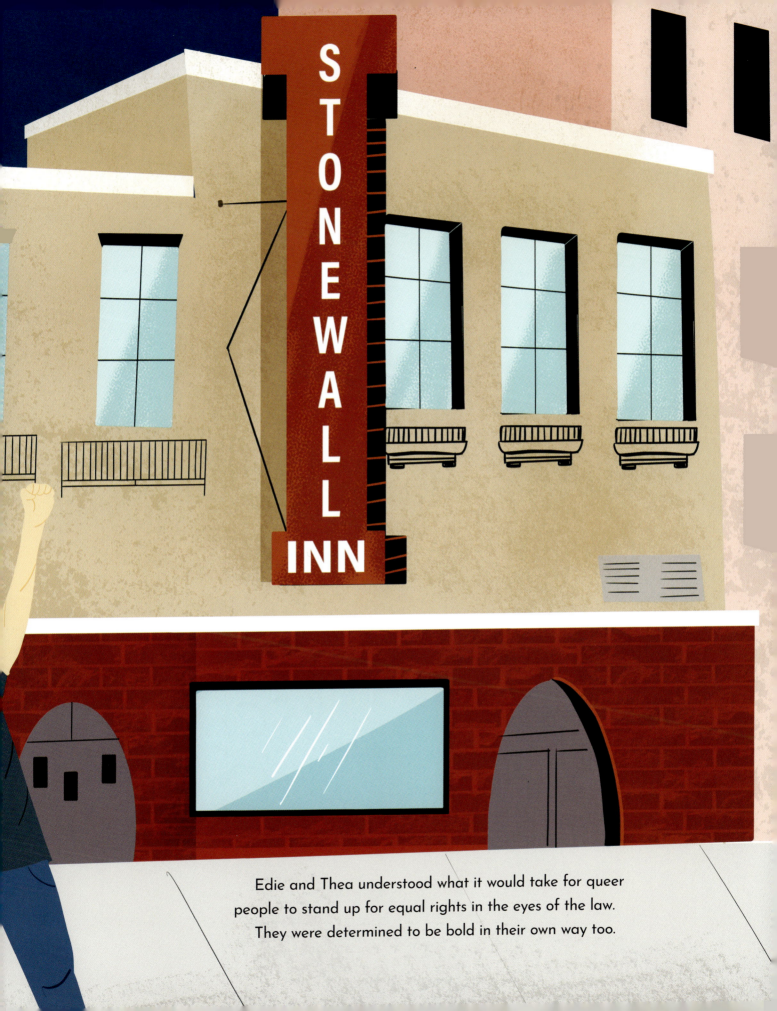

Edie and Thea understood what it would take for queer people to stand up for equal rights in the eyes of the law. They were determined to be bold in their own way too.

But being bold wasn't going to be easy. Their own families disapproved of gay and lesbian relationships, and Edie and Thea did not feel free to be a couple around them.

So they created a loving family of wonderful friends who inspired them to stand up for equal rights.

Edie and Thea showed up at protests and volunteered at local community organizations that supported queer people.

With her computer smarts, Edie even helped these organizations solve their technology problems!

Over the years, Thea began having problems with her knee whenever she and Edie danced. She started falling for no reason.

Doctors told Thea she had a condition that would make using her arms and legs difficult. As Thea's health grew worse and she could no longer walk on her own, Edie quit her job to take care of her.

Despite the hardships, Edie and Thea kept dancing and told each other, "Never postpone joy!"

And they never did. Forty years after their engagement, they got married! It wasn't legal for them to marry in their home state of New York, so with the help of their chosen family they flew to Canada, where it was legal. There were lots of tears of joy and tissues.

There was no more hiding.

Two years later, their joy came to an end when Thea passed away. Edie's heart was broken. She calculated that their love had lasted 382,872 hours, 15,953 days—nearly 44 years!

Then one day Edie opened a letter from the US government. It was an inheritance tax bill for more than three hundred thousand dollars!

Edie knew this was unfair. A wife could inherit property and money from a husband without paying any tax, but this bill meant that the government did not recognize the marriages between wives and wives or husbands and husbands.

First Edie was shocked, and then she got mad. She yelled, "How can you treat us differently?! How can you treat *her* differently?!"

Edie wanted the world to know: "If Thea was a Theo, I wouldn't have had to pay!" The tax bill was unequal. The math did not add up.

There was only one thing to do: Edie sued the US government.

People warned Edie that it was not the right time for lesbian and gay people to fight for their rights.

Edie didn't listen. It was her time to stand up for what was right, even if Thea wasn't there to be bold with her.

Edie contacted several lawyers, but no one would represent her. At last, Edie met attorney Roberta "Robbie" Kaplan. Being lesbian, Robbie had also experienced unfairness in her life.

She also knew Thea. Some years earlier, Thea had been Robbie's therapist. She had helped Robbie see that she could have a loving relationship, just like Edie and Thea.

Robbie was determined to help Edie.

Robbie knew Edie had a strong case. The law they had to defeat was called the "Defense of Marriage Act," also known as DOMA. The particular part of the law Edie and Robbie were fighting against was the definition of marriage. According to DOMA, the US government recognized marriage only between a man and a woman.

Robbie told reporters that the way to win the case was to convince the justices on the Supreme Court and other Americans that "Edie and Thea's marriage was the same as anyone else's marriage, and that they had the same right to be treated with dignity as anyone else."

The first step was to argue Edie's case in a lower court, where all cases begin. After many months and arguments, the court made its decision.

The court agreed with Robbie and Edie that DOMA did not treat people equally. DOMA was on its way to being removed as a law!

But the US government didn't agree with the lower court and took it to a higher court, hoping to keep the law in place.

Robbie and Edie were ready! A few months later, Robbie argued the case before the new court.

And guess what? Edie won again! The higher court also agreed that DOMA was not right, not fair, and not equal.

Edie and Robbie knew the fight was not over and that the government would try again to keep the unfair law.

So this time Robbie argued the case before the Supreme Court of the United States—the highest court in the country.

In *United States v. Windsor*, 570 U.S. 744 (2013), Robbie stood before nine Supreme Court justices and argued, "Gay married couples' relationships are not significantly different from the relationships of straight married people." Robbie shared that Edie and Thea had loved each other for close to forty-four years,

in sickness and in health. But now Edie was being told that her marriage wasn't real and was being treated differently.

That, Robbie argued, was called discrimination. It was unfair. Unequal.

When Edie and Robbie left the Supreme Court, a wild roar erupted from the crowd outside with people shouting, "Edie, Edie!"

Three months later, the Supreme Court justices reached their decision. They agreed—DOMA was unconstitutional! The US government had to treat Edie and Thea's marriage like all other legal marriages.

Though she was tiny in stature, Edie had become a giant symbol for equality at eighty-four years old. Standing on the shoulders of so many activists who came before her, Edie Windsor helped her country fix a great unfairness.

Although the fight for equal rights continues, Edie proved that love is love, that equal means equal.

And that adds up every time.

TIMELINE OF LEGAL AND SOCIETAL EVENTS LEADING UP TO AND FOLLOWING *UNITED STATES V. WINDSOR*

1868: The Fourteenth Amendment grants citizenship to all persons born or naturalized in the United States, including formerly enslaved people, and provides all citizens "equal protection under the laws."

1929: Edith "Edie" Schlain is born in Philadelphia, PA, to Celia and James Schlain. She later adopts the last name Windsor in 1951, while briefly married to a man.

1931: Thea Clara Spyer is born in Amsterdam, Holland; as a young child, Thea moves with her family to England (and then America), fleeing the Nazis.

1950: The Mattachine Society is founded as a national gay rights organization in the United States.

1951: Edie moves to New York City to start a new life and embrace being lesbian.

1953: President Dwight D. Eisenhower signs Executive Order 10450, revising security standards for federal employment, banning gays and lesbians from working for the federal government. Following this order, thousands of federal employees are fired on suspicion of being gay.

1958: *One, Inc v. Olesen* is one of the first Supreme Court of the United States (SCOTUS) cases that considers the civil rights of LGBTQ people. SCOTUS validates that people have the right to publish LGBTQ media.

1963: Edie and Thea meet at Portofino, a restaurant in New York City.

1966: A riot occurs at Compton's Cafeteria in the Tenderloin neighborhood of San Francisco due to unrelenting police harassment of drag queens and trans people. This riot is one of several that take place across the US.

1967: Edie and Thea become engaged—for what would be a very long engagement (over forty years!).

1969: The Stonewall Uprising (also called the Stonewall Riots) occurs in Greenwich Village, New York City. In the early morning of June 28, police raid the gay club Stonewall Inn following several previous raids. This leads to several days of protests and unrest and becomes known as the spark for the gay rights movement in the United States and the world.

After Stonewall, many activists join together to form the Gay Liberation Front (GLF).

1970: Activists Marsha P. Johnson and Sylvia Rivera leave GLF to form STAR (Street Transvestite Action Revolutionaries) to help provide housing and support to LGBT people in need.

The first Christopher Street Gay Liberation Day March is held in New York City on June 28, the one-year anniversary of the Stonewall Uprising.

1972: SCOTUS considers the issue of marriage equality for the first time, in *Baker v. Nelson*. A gay couple wants to marry in Minnesota. SCOTUS dismisses the case, noting this is a state issue.

1986: In *Bowers v. Hardwick*, SCOTUS decides that the Fourteenth Amendment does not prevent a state from criminalizing the private lives of same-sex couples.

1990: Mary Bonauto becomes the first civil rights lawyer for GLAD (Gay and Lesbian Advocates and Defenders) and will later lead some of the first strategic challenges to Section 3 of DOMA. She is referred to as a "gay marriage hero."

1991: In *Baehr v. Miike* (originally *Baehr v. Lewin*), three LGBTQ couples sue to force the state of Hawaii to issue them marriage licenses. Rulings in 1993 and 1996 by Hawaii state courts create momentum for same-sex couples to be able to marry. Eventually, in 1999, a Hawaii state constitutional amendment allows the state to limit marriage to opposite-sex couples and leads to a dismissal of the case.

1993: Under the Clinton administration, the US military adopts the "Don't Ask, Don't Tell" policy, barring openly gay, lesbian, and bisexual individuals from serving.

1996: President Bill Clinton signs into law the Defense of Marriage Act (DOMA), which states in Section 3 that marriage is between "a man and a woman" and bars the federal government from recognizing gay and lesbian marriages.

SCOTUS rules in *Romer v. Evans* that laws cannot single out LGBTQ people to deny them rights.

1999: In *Baker v. Vermont*, the Vermont Supreme Court rules that same-sex couples cannot be excluded from the benefits and protections that the state provides to opposite-sex married couples. Mary Bonauto represents the three same-sex couples who had been denied marriage licenses in the state.

2000: Vermont becomes the first state to legalize same-sex civil unions.

In *Boy Scouts of America v. Dale*, SCOTUS rules that a private organization could single out LGBTQ people to disallow their membership.

2003: In *Goodridge et al. v. Department of Public Health*, Mary Bonauto represents seven same-sex couples wanting to marry in Massachusetts. Massachusetts becomes the first state to grant same-sex marriage.

Lawrence v. Texas overrules the earlier SCOTUS decision in *Bowers v. Hardwick*, declaring that LGBTQ people could not be criminalized for their loving relationships, setting the stage for federally recognized same-sex marriage as a possibility.

Evan Wolfson, a longtime marriage equality advocate, launches Freedom to Marry, an organization that establishes a strategy to achieve marriage for same-sex couples nationwide. He becomes known as the "godfather of gay marriage."

2004: San Francisco mayor Gavin Newsom allows same-sex couples to marry in the city. One month later, the California Supreme Court puts a halt to these marriages and makes the four thousand marriage licenses issued invalid, ruling that the mayor did not have the authority to change the state law that banned them.

2007: Seventy-seven-year old Edie and seventy-five-year old Thea marry in Toronto, Canada, with their friend Harvey Brownstone, the first openly gay judge in Canada, presiding.

2008: In May, the California Supreme Court finds that barring same-sex couples from marriage violates the California constitution. In June, when same-sex couples can be issued marriage licenses in California, an estimated eighteen thousand couples marry. Then in November, Proposition 8, which amends the California state constitution to prohibit same-sex marriage, passes.

2009: Thea dies peacefully at age seventy-seven from aortic stenosis. Edie receives a federal tax bill of $363,053 and a New York State bill of $275,528.

2010: Edie's attorney, Roberta "Robbie" Kaplan, files her case with the Southern District of New York. Edie is eighty years old.

2011: President Barack Obama and his administration consider DOMA to be unconstitutional and order the Department of Justice to stop defending it. In this same year, New York State legalizes same-sex marriage, and the US military's "Don't Ask, Don't Tell" policy is repealed.

2012: On June 6, in *Windsor v. United States*, the Southern District of New York (SDNY) Judge Barbara Jones rules that DOMA, Section 3, is unconstitutional. On October 18, the Second Circuit Court of Appeals upholds the SDNY ruling. SCOTUS agrees to hear Edie's case.

In *Gill v. Office of Personnel Management*, the United States Court of Appeals for the First Circuit affirms a lower court decision that Section 3 of DOMA is unconstitutional.

2013: Former president Bill Clinton writes an op-ed in the *Washington Post* entitled "It's time to overturn DOMA." He acknowledges the law he originally signed in 1996 was discriminatory against gay and lesbian couples.

On March 27, 2013, Robbie Kaplan presents Edie's case before SCOTUS in *United States v. Windsor*. On June 26, the court issues their 5-4 ruling that Section 3 of DOMA is unconstitutional. Edie and Robbie win their case. Writing the majority opinion, Justice Anthony Kennedy emphasizes that Edie's case was about human dignity and equality.

In *Hollingsworth v. Perry* SCOTUS upholds an appeals court ruling that Proposition 8 violated the Fourteenth Amendment.

2015: On June 26, SCOTUS rules in *Obergefell v. Hodges* that Section 2 of DOMA is unconstitutional and, because of the Fourteenth Amendment, all states must grant same-sex marriages and recognize same-sex marriages from other states.

2016: Edie Windsor marries Judith Kasen on September 26 in New York City.

2017: At the age of eighty-eight, Edie Windsor dies on September 12 in Manhattan.

2018: In *Masterpiece Cakeshop, Ltd v. Colorado Civil Rights Commission*, SCOTUS finds that a baker cannot be required to make wedding cakes for same-sex marriages if the baker opposes same-sex marriage for religious reasons.

2022: On December 12, President Joe Biden signs the Respect for Marriage Act, requiring all states to recognize same-sex and interracial marriages performed in other states and federally recognizes these marriages. The law officially voids DOMA.

2023: New York City honors Edie Windsor and Thea Spyer by co-naming Fifth Avenue and Washington Square North (where they once lived) "Edie Windsor and Thea Spyer Way" on June 20.

DEFENSE OF MARRIAGE ACT (DOMA)

The Defense of Marriage Act (DOMA) was passed in 1996 and signed into law by President Bill Clinton. It consisted of three sections. The first was just a title, but the second two were the important parts. Section 2 said that no US state (or US territory, US possession, or Native American tribe) had to recognize a same-sex marriage from another state. This was in stark contrast to how states were mandated to recognize opposite-sex marriages from other states. Then Section 3 defined the mention of marriage in any federal law to mean only a legal union between a man and a woman.

Edie Windsor's case, *United States v. Windsor*, was about overturning Section 3 of DOMA because the law allowed the federal government to discriminate against married lesbian and gay couples (from the nine states plus the District of Columbia that recognized same-sex marriage at the time the *Windsor* case was heard), treating them as unequal to straight married couples. This discrimination included gay and lesbian couples being denied hundreds of federal benefits provided to straight married couples, including: filing taxes jointly, having no inheritance taxes owed by a surviving spouse, and unpaid leave to care for a sick or injured spouse.

In *United States v. Windsor*, the Supreme Court ruled that Section 3 was unconstitutional. This meant that the federal government must recognize any same-sex marriage performed in a state where same-sex marriage was legal. Since only Section 3 was under review in the *United States v. Windsor* decision, states could still choose not to recognize legal marriages from other states. However, the reasoning that was used by the Supreme Court would set the stage two years later for the challenge to Section 2 in *Obergefell v. Hodges*, when same-sex marriage was made the law of the land.

Edie Windsor (r) and Thea Spyer (l) in their Greenwich Village home.
©NEVILLE ELDER/GETTY IMAGES

WHAT IS THE SUPREME COURT OF THE UNITED STATES?

The Supreme Court of the United States (SCOTUS) is the highest court in the nation. SCOTUS's ultimate responsibility is inscribed on the building where the court is located: equal justice under law. As the top court, SCOTUS has the last say on all cases that involve federal laws. The decisions of SCOTUS are final and cannot be appealed. There are nine justices (or judges), including a chief justice. They are appointed by the president and confirmed by the Senate whenever there is a vacancy. Justices are appointed for life and serve until they resign, retire, are impeached, or die. SCOTUS receives over seven thousand requests a year to review cases but only about a hundred to a hundred and fifty of these are presented to them each year (they are in session from October to June). These cases affect the entire country and can have a big impact by setting policies that result in real social change. After hearing a case, the justices reach a decision, with each judge having a single vote. When five justices or more agree on an outcome, that is called a majority. The chief justice or the most senior justice (meaning the judge who has been on the Supreme Court the longest) in the majority decides who will write up the decision (or opinion). The minority also writes the reason they disagree (or their dissent).

SCOTUS and the rest of the court system

(the judicial branch) comprise one of the three equal branches of government, along with the Congress (the legislative branch) and the president (the executive branch). SCOTUS has the power to determine whether laws passed by Congress or actions taken by the president violate the Constitution and are deemed not legal or not valid.

HOW DOES A CASE REACH THE UNITED STATES SUPREME COURT?

There are two court systems: state courts, which deal with state laws; and federal courts that handle national laws. The Supreme Court is part of the federal court system.

The federal court system has three levels: district, appeals, and supreme courts. Most cases start out at the lowest level, at one of the ninety-four district courts around the country. Judges and juries listen to the arguments from both sides of the dispute and sometimes hear from witnesses. The juries reach a decision (called a verdict) in favor of one side or the other. Judges give rulings about the law.

If either side believes the district court verdict or some of the rulings are wrong, the case can be taken to the middle level, at one of the twelve appeals courts around the country. Appeals courts do not have juries or witnesses, only judges who determine whether the law was applied correctly in the district court. Most decisions of the appeals courts end there, but those decisions can be appealed to the highest court, the Supreme Court in Washington, DC.

The Supreme Court tends to hear cases for which there are conflicting lower court rulings or when there is an issue of law that has not been resolved (including the possibility that a previous Supreme Court ruling could be wrong). As in the appeals courts, there are no witnesses or jury at the Supreme Court—and the justices ultimately determine whether the law has been interpreted and applied correctly.

EDIE WINDSOR GOES TO WASHINGTON, DC

Edith Windsor had never set out to become an activist. In fact, quite the opposite: as she discovered her attraction to other women, she also learned that this had to stay hidden or risk losing family, friends, or employment. But then, in 1963, Edie met Thea and fell in love. That's all Edie wanted: to find love, to be loved, and for this love to be accepted and respected. And that's exactly what she ended up fighting for in *United States v. Windsor*. Together for nearly forty-four years, legally married their last two years together, and coping with Thea's long battle with MS, they had a relationship that was a testament to the power of love. Despite their long-standing commitment to each other, Edie faced a large inheritance tax bill after Thea passed away. Fueled by love for Thea and an upswelling of anger and feelings of unfairness, Edie stood up and shifted from that quiet, timid young woman to a bold, vocal activist. It resulted in Edie becoming a very visible face of modern-day gay and lesbian rights when she sued the United States government to repeal Section 3 of the Defense of Marriage Act (DOMA).

Following the arguments in *United States v. Windsor* at the Supreme Court came the waiting for the official ruling. While the team of lawyers felt confident that the ruling would

Embracing a cheering crowd, Edie leaves the Supreme Court following oral arguments challenging DOMA.
© PETE MAROVICH/ZUMAPRESS.COM/ALAMY

be favorable, for many others, patiently waiting was understandably a difficult process. And then the ruling came during New York City's annual gay pride celebration. Edie was at Robbie Kaplan's home on the day the ruling was released: Section 3 of DOMA was unconstitutional. As soon as they read the ruling, Edie, Robbie, and friends shouted, cried, and jumped up and down. President Obama called Edie to thank her for speaking out and making such a difference in the country.

Edie wanted to go to the Stonewall Inn, known as a major site of modern-day gay rights activism, to celebrate the victory. At Stonewall, hundreds of people had gathered in excitement and love. Other celebrations included a fabulous dance party, honoring Thea and Edie's lifetime of dancing together. Edie was also the Grand Marshal of the New York City LGBTQ+ Pride Parade and was a runner-up (to winner Pope Francis) for *Time* magazine's Person of the Year.

WHY WAS *UNITED STATES V. WINDSOR* IMPORTANT, AND WHAT IMPACT HAS IT HAD GOING FORWARD?

On June 26, 2013, SCOTUS delivered their 5-4 ruling: Section 3 of DOMA was unfair and unconstitutional. Edie was refunded the taxes she had paid. More important, she got the US government to recognize gay and lesbian marriages in the states where they were already legal—equal protection under the law. *United States v. Windsor* was a huge gay rights victory. In Justice Anthony Kennedy's majority opinion, he used the word "dignity" (a word that means worthy of honor and respect) nine times. He wrote that, "interference with the equal dignity of same-sex marriages was more than an incidental effect of DOMA. It was its essence." He added that DOMA had written inequality into the United States Code. Edie's case, therefore, was about bringing dignity and equality to married same-sex couples and their children and families.

United States v. Windsor was also about reversing discrimination against gay and lesbian couples. It paved the way for *Obergefell v. Hodges*, a US Supreme Court case that was decided two years later, in 2015. Like Edie and Thea, Jim Obergefell had been in a long-term relationship. Jim married his partner, John Arthur, in Maryland shortly before John died of Lou Gehrig's disease. But they lived in Ohio (where it was not yet legal to marry), and Jim wanted his marriage to John to be legal in their home state. His case was challenging Section 2 of DOMA, which said that one US state did not have to recognize the marriage of a same-sex couple that took place in another state.

On June 26, 2015, SCOTUS made same-sex marriage legal *everywhere* in the country. In his majority opinion, Justice Kennedy emphasized this point: "In forming a marital union, two people become greater than they once were. As some of the petitioners in these cases demonstrate, marriage embodies a love that may endure even past death. . . . They ask for equal dignity in the eyes of the law. The Constitution grants them that right. . . . It is so ordered."

AUTHOR'S NOTE

Growing up as a gay kid, I vividly remember witnessing a few boys being teased and beaten up mercilessly just for being themselves in high school. Seeing this, I stayed away from those boys—which did not feel right at all.

Later, in college and graduate school, I came out as gay, thankfully to a supportive group of friends. My family, however, was very lukewarm. They didn't know what to make of it, and their silence felt like an unspoken disapproval. I felt alone. Then I met John, who would later become my husband, and we started our lives together in Washington, DC, and then we moved to San Francisco.

Like many couples, John and I thought about starting a family. In 1995, it wasn't common for an openly gay couple to adopt children. In fact, in many states same-sex couples were banned from adopting children. We were lucky though and met our daughter's birth mother when she was four months pregnant. Our daughter, Gabby, was born on Christmas Day, and her birth mother handed the baby to us in a bright red stocking. We cried many tears of joy. Having a baby brought us closer to our families of origin; Gabby, appealing and delightful, was a kind of bridge to our relatives, who could relate to all the wonder of having children.

In September 2008, John and I got married during a brief window of time when it was legal in California. Gabby, age twelve, gave us away and stole the show with her singing and guitar playing. John's family flew out from Washington, DC, to join us in celebrating,

Channeling Edie's joy at the site of her history-changing victory. PHOTO COURTESY OF THE AUTHOR.

but upsettingly, no one from my Southern California family was present. It felt pretty awful. Despite this hurt, surrounded by chosen family, our wedding day gave us an enormous feeling of legitimacy—just as it had for Edie and Thea. It felt like equality was finally within reach.

But very sadly, on November 5, 2008, California passed Proposition 8, and gay and lesbian couples could no longer marry in the state. Like many others, we felt this was the continuation of a great inequality. So when Edie Windsor took her case to the US Supreme Court to fight for love and equality, there was hope again. Edie inspired me to use my voice to stand up for marriage equality and love for all. And it is my hope that everyone who reads about Edie and her fight will be inspired to find their own boldness in standing up for fairness and equality too.

My husband, John Stiehler (l), officiant and friend James Schurz (c), and me (r) on our wedding day. PHOTO COURTESY OF THE AUTHOR.